MACBETH THE Red King

SHAUN MANNING
story and words

ANNA WIESZCZYK
artwork and colors

ALLYSON HALLER
collection design

MACBETH: THE RED KING

© SHAUN MANNING & BLUE FOX PUBLISHING

Published by Blue Fox Publishing Limited
bluefoxcomics.com

Blue Fox Comics and its logos are registered trademarks and copyrights of Blue Fox Publishing Limited. All rights reserved. No part of this publication may be reproduced or transmitted, in any form or by any means (except for short excerpts for review purposes) without the express permission of Shaun Manning and Blue Fox Publishing Limited.

All names, characters, events, and locales in this publication, except for historical purposes, are entirely fictional. Artworks, images, and character likenesses herein are copyright Shaun Manning and Blue Fox Publishing Limited.

INTRODUCTION

This is not the "true story" of Macbeth. But neither was the immortal play. Macbeth: The Red King is a story of Macbeth, drawn from contemporary sources much the way William Shakespeare would have done. The Scottish Play has been an overwhelmingly dominant narrative of the early 11th century king for more than 400 years – it tells us that Macbeth was an usurper and tyrant, that he murdered the beloved King Duncan in his sleep, that his ambition was spurred on by dark forces. Shakespeare chose to tell a particular story – he did alright with it. I'm choosing to tell a different one.

We don't know a lot about the "real" Macbeth (or Mac bethad, a Christian name meaning "Son of Life"). Historical records were not as robust, those that existed were prone to bias, there are many conflicting accounts regarding major events and familial relationships, and of course much is likely to be lost over the course of a thousand years. But what we do know suggests old Bill Shakes got a few things wrong. Never mind the witches, Banquo and Fleance are also pure inventions. Duncan definitely did not die in his sleep, nor was he a wizened old ruler; he was probably in his twenties. Lady Macbeth famously mentions having "given suck," yet her son is nowhere to be found in the drama. Those were choices Shakespeare made.

From what we know, too, it's not at all clear Macbeth was the usurper he's been reviled as for the last millennium. Before Malcolm II, Duncan's grandfather and immediate predecessor, the Scottish monarchy operated on a system of alternating succession between two related families; under this system, Macbeth likely had a better claim on the throne than did Duncan. Gruoch ("Lady Macbeth") was also of royal stock, making this pair born for the role. Malcolm II naming his own grandson to succeed him broke the cycle, then Duncan made it worse by trying to assert his authority over Macbeth's domain.

And for all that, Macbeth was probably a pretty good king. He ruled for more than 15 years during a volatile period; during this time, we know that he travelled to Rome, where he gave alms to the poor and very likely met with the pope. This was not a short journey in the mid-eleventh century; there was no RyanAir. That he returned to find his kingdom intact is strong evidence that he couldn't have been the monster portrayed in the play. What did people say about him in his own time? The best we can do is look at a few near-contemporary accounts, like the Prophecy of Berchan, which dates to a few generations after Macbeth's death – the author says, "he will be pleasant to me among them; Scotland will be brimful west and east during the reign of the furious red one." Another small mention, written within a couple hundred years of Macbeth's reign, describes him as "a demon." Either or both could have been politically motivated. Who knows. Shakespeare had good motivation for playing Macbeth as the villain, since King James VI of Scotland, who had just become King James I of England, was a direct descendent of Malcolm. III. I am not, so far as I know, in any way related to any of the historical characters in this comic.

Shakespeare made choices; I made others. My story hews a bit closer to the skeletal timeline we have of Macbeth's life, but that doesn't make it "true." Major events are skipped over, others are embellished. There is no evidence that Malcolm III was the little snot I've portrayed him as, but god was he fun to write. Lulach's grudge toward his stepfather is likewise my own invention, though the circumstances of how this family was formed are fairly accurate. Thorfinn is a puzzle; he's got two Norse epics written about him, one of which features an ongoing struggle with a King of Scots who can pretty much only be Macbeth. Neither account is especially reliable, though, and anyway leaning on these two much would distract from the main story. His role here is to represent a powerful neighbor, someone who is not a friend but may, with luck, be an ally. Macbeth does not have that good luck.

As every production of Shakespeare's The Tragedy of Macbeth is unique, I have to thank artist Anna Wieszczyk for so brilliantly staging Macbeth: The Red King. Costume, scenery, acting, it's all to her credit.

Will our story of Macbeth survive 400 years and counting? Man, wouldn't that be nice? I will be satisfied if you, as readers, enjoy the book, if it helps you think about one of Shakespeare's most famous works, if it deepens your interest in history and how history is constructed. Thank you for reading.

SHAUN MANNING
April 2018

ACT I
The King of Moray

ELGIN CATHEDRAL! HURRY, TO SANCTUARY!

THEY'RE ALL INSIDE. SHALL WE SURROUND THE CHURCH?

NO.

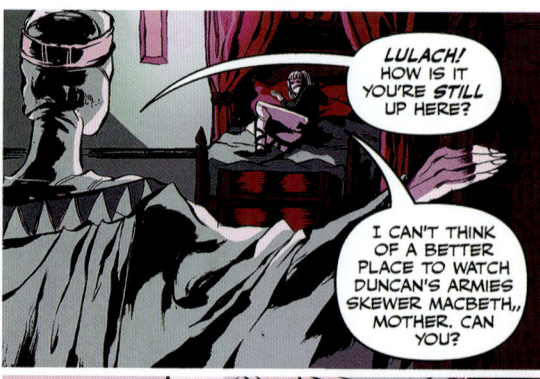

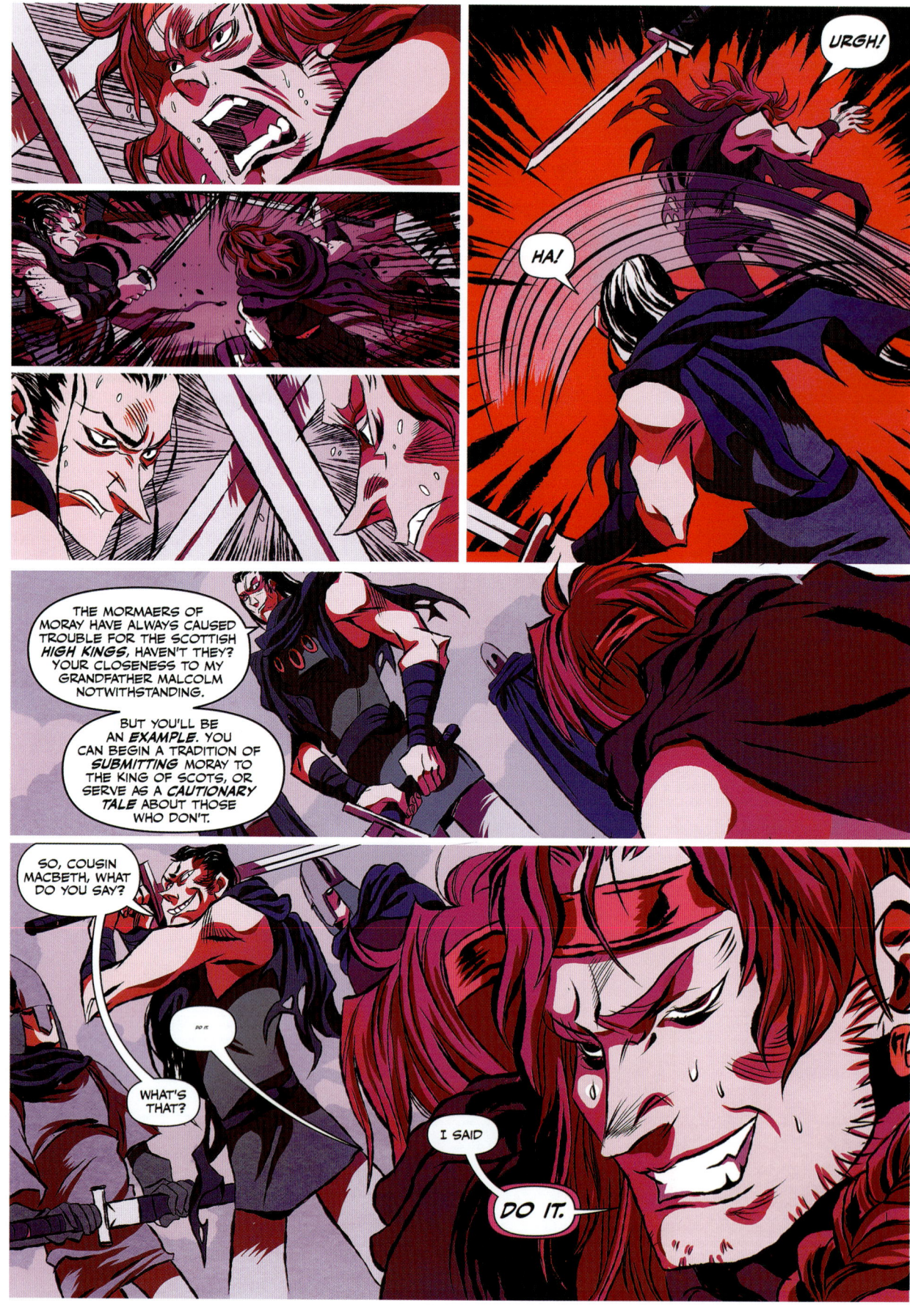

"YOU'RE REALLY GOING, EH? LEAVING ME HERE, WASTING AWAY."

"AYE, I'VE GOT TO GO. *HIS HOLINESS THE POPE* HAS AGREED TO SEE ME, I CAN'T VERY WELL SAY NO.

I'LL BE BACK BEFORE YOU CAN MISS ME."

"DON'T COUNT ON IT."

ROME.

ACT III
Siege

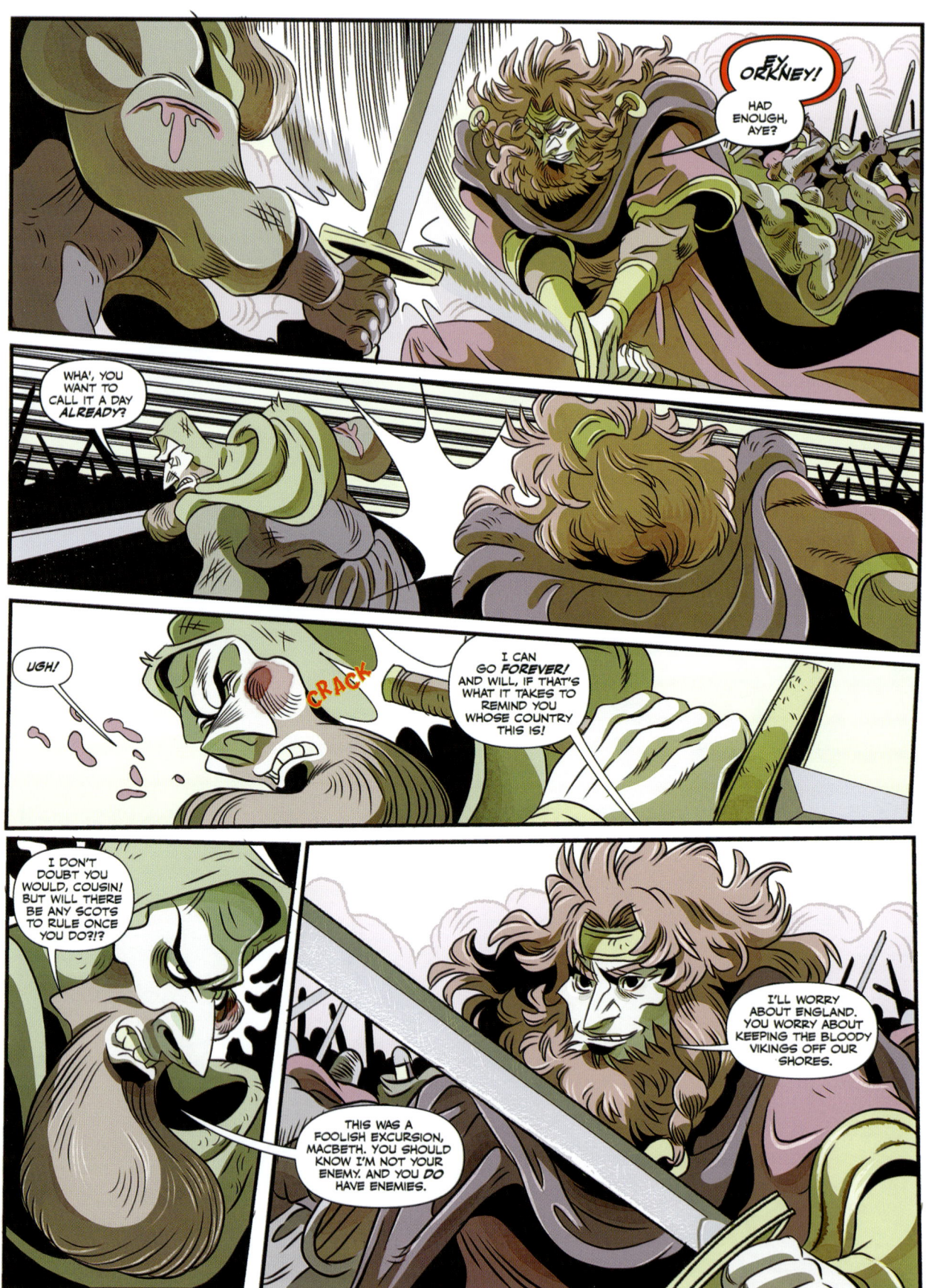

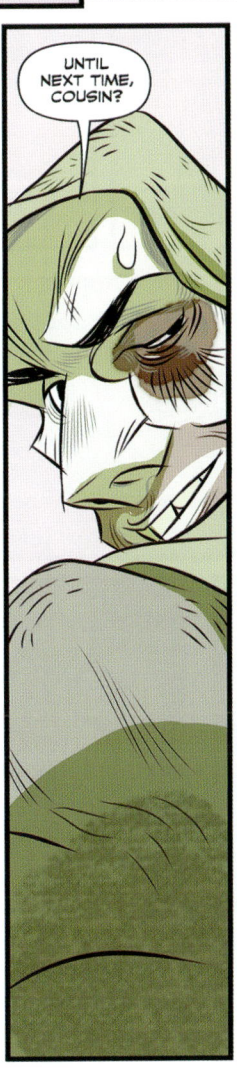

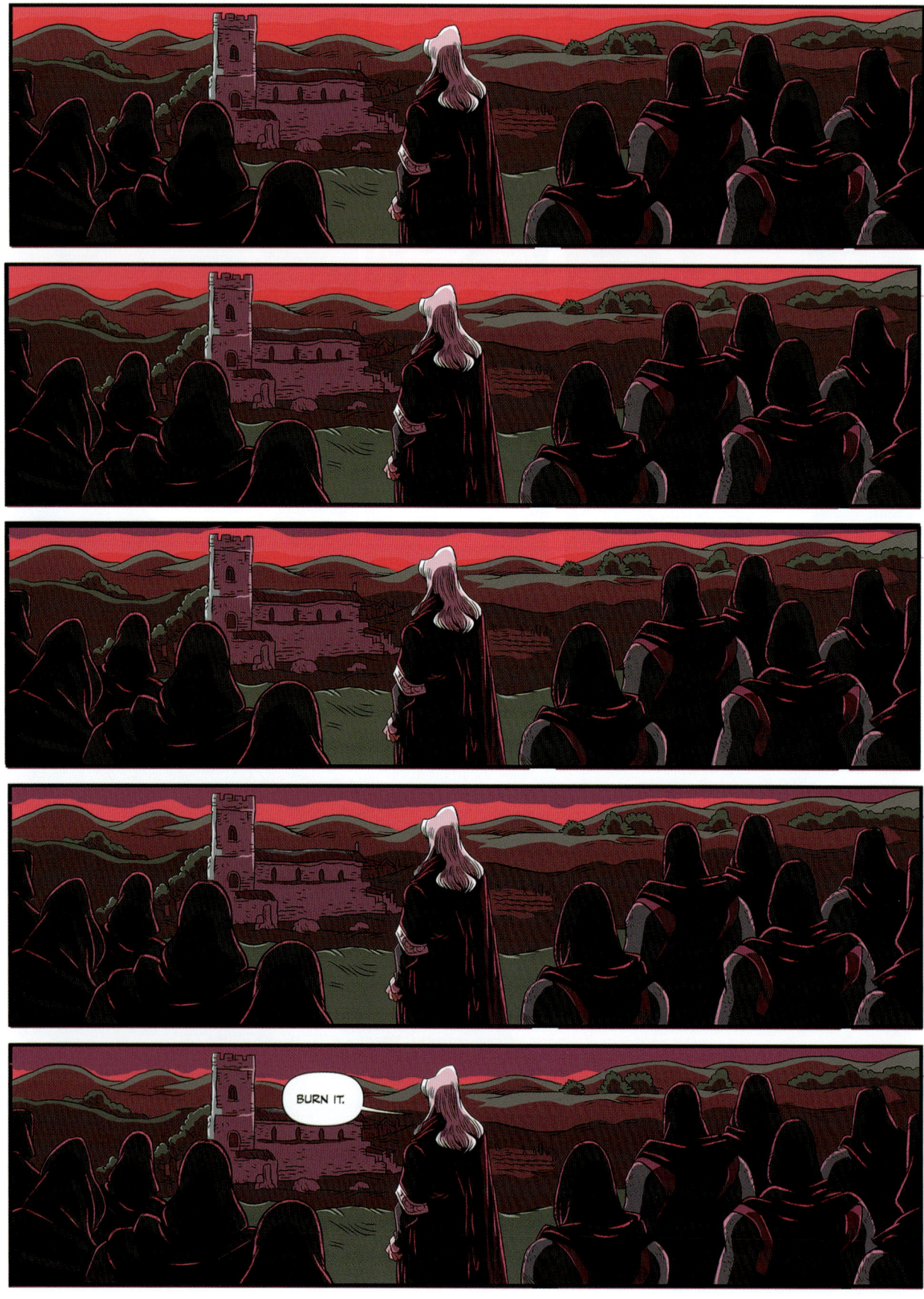

IT'S OVER.